The Last King of Scotland

GILES FODEN

Level 3

Retold by Chris Rice
Series Editors: Andy Hopkins and Jocelyn Potter

Pearson Education Limited
Edinburgh Gate, Harlow,
Essex CM20 2JE, England
and Associated Companies throughout the world.

ISBN: 978-1-4082-6379-2

This edition first published by Pearson Education Ltd 2012

3 5 7 9 10 8 6 4 2

Original copyright © Giles Foden 1998
Text copyright © Pearson Education Ltd 2012
Illustrations by Dragon76

Set in 11/14pt Bembo
Printed in China
SWTC/02

The moral right of the author has been asserted in accordance with
the Copyright Designs and Patents Act 1988

Published by Pearson Education Limited in association with
Penguin Books Ltd, and both companies being subsidiaries of Pearson PLC

For a complete list of the titles available in the Penguin Readers series please go to
www.penguinreaders.com. Alternatively, write to your local Pearson Longman office
or to: Penguin Readers Marketing Department, Pearson Education,
Edinburgh Gate, Harlow, Essex CM20 2JE, England.

Contents

Introduction

I checked his chest and stomach, touching him softly and nervously. Surprisingly, as I moved my hands over his body, I had a very strange feeling … A strong, mysterious power seemed to move, through my fingers, from his body into mine.

It is the early 1970s and Nicholas Garrigan, a young Scottish doctor, is working in a small clinic near the town of Mbarara in the west of Uganda. In his first job after leaving university, he is enjoying the adventure of life in a strange, foreign country. Then, one day, there is a car accident not far from the clinic, and Garrigan's help is needed. When he arrives, a man is lying in the road. But this is not an ordinary man – it is the President of Uganda, Idi Amin. After this meeting, Garrigan's life will never be the same. This is the powerful and unforgettable story of an ordinary man who becomes the personal doctor – and close friend – of one of the most dangerous and hated men in the world.

Idi Amin was president of Uganda from 1971 to 1979. At first, he received help from many countries – the UK, Israel, South Africa, Libya, and the Soviet Union. But during his time as president, he did many terrible, crazy things, and between 100,000 and 500,000 Ugandans died. He left Uganda after starting a war with Tanzania. He died in Saudi Arabia in 2003.

Giles Foden was born in England in 1967. From the age of five until his early twenties, he lived with his family in many different African countries. *The Last King of Scotland* (1998) was an immediate success, and a film of the story was made in 2006, with Forest Whitaker as Idi Amin.

Chapter 1 A Strong, Mysterious Power

I was working as a doctor in the south-west of Uganda, near the town of Mbarara, when I first met Idi Amin. The President of Uganda enjoyed driving his red Maserati at top speed along the narrow country roads. One day he drove his sports car into a cow and was thrown out onto the road. He sent his soldiers for a doctor, and they came to the clinic in Mbarara, the nearest town. There they found me, and brought me to him by the roadside.

The cow was lying on one side of the road, making a terrible noise. It was clearly in great pain. Behind it, with one wheel off the road, was the red Maserati, with its front knocked badly out of shape. On the other side of the road, lying on his back with one hand in the air, was Idi Amin.

Meeting him in person for the first time, I was surprised by his great size. Even lying on his back by the roadside he seemed larger than life. He wasn't badly hurt, except for his wrist. I tied some cloth tightly around it. Then I checked his chest and stomach, touching him softly and nervously. Surprisingly, as I moved my hands over his body, I had a very strange feeling. I began to feel weak and light-headed. A strong, mysterious power seemed to move, through my fingers, from his body into mine.

'My dear Doctor Garrigan,' he said at the end of my examination, pulling himself to his feet with his good hand on my shoulder. 'Thank you very much. Let us drink to your success.'

A soldier brought two bottles of beer from the Maserati. Amin took the bottles and handed one to me. 'You know,' he said with a laugh, 'every president has a bar in his car. Good health!'

1

He drank his beer quickly. I drank mine nervously. I couldn't believe what was happening. I was drinking on a small country road on a burning hot day, next to a bright red sports car and a dying cow – with Idi Amin!

I realised that Amin was studying me closely.

'This is excellent beer,' I said.

Suddenly, I heard the sound of a gunshot and I jumped with fear. I looked around quickly. A soldier was walking away from the cow, a gun in his hand.

'Do not be afraid,' Amin smiled. 'He has just put the cow out of its pain.'

'Poor thing,' I said.

'It is only meat ... The soldiers can have it for dinner tonight.'

We stood in silence for a few seconds, and then he looked at me seriously. 'I would like to thank you again for your help,' he said. He reached into his pocket and pulled out a handful of money. 'This is for you.'

I stepped back. 'No, I couldn't possibly ...' I said.

'Skill means money, Doctor Garrigan. Take it.'

'But I didn't do anything.'

He looked at me quietly for a second. I was worried that he was angry with me. Then, with a thoughtful look on his face, he said, 'Perhaps you should work for me in Kampala. You will be well paid. You are clearly very intelligent. Well, I am too. But everyone is intelligent in different ways.'

'I'm happy in my job here,' I said.

'All right,' he said. 'But I will still speak to my Minister of Health about it. Now I have to go and speak to the chiefs in this area. They are not very modern. They are slow to understand. I have to tell them everything twice.' He straightened his back and looked down at me from his great height. 'Well, goodbye, Doctor, and thank you again.'

With a wide smile he got into his vehicle. 'Doctor

Garrigan!' He called me to him. 'I will see you again.' As he looked up at me from the low driving seat of his car, I saw something mysterious – half-frightening, half-wonderful – in his eyes. 'Remember this when you make your decision,' he said: 'Water runs down into a valley; it does not climb a hill.'

With those words, he quickly drove away.

A few months later, I received an invitation from the Minister of Health, Jonah Wasswa, to become Idi Amin's personal doctor in the Ugandan capital, Kampala.

Chapter 2 The Clinic at Mbarara

Two years before that first strange meeting with Idi Amin, I was an ordinary young man in Scotland looking for his first job after university. But I didn't want a boring job as a doctor in my own country. I was young and I wanted adventure. I wanted to see the world. So when I was offered a job at a small clinic in Uganda, I accepted it immediately.

I arrived at Entebbe airport with one suitcase and £300 in my pocket. No one was waiting for me, so I took a taxi to Kampala. I booked into a small hotel and, after a shower, I went down to the bar. There, I met a large, strong white man with a black beard.

'My name's Freddy Swanepoel,' he said, lighting a cigarette. I could tell from his voice that he was South African.

'Nicholas Garrigan,' I replied, shaking hands with him.

'What are you doing in Kampala?'

'I'm a doctor.'

'There'll be plenty of work for you here,' he said.

'And what do *you* do?' I asked him.

'I'm a pilot. I carry things for the Kenyan and Ugandan governments.' He drank some beer. 'And I do a few other jobs,' he added thoughtfully.

The conversation moved to the political situation. 'There's going to be trouble,' he said. 'The army is going to take power. But don't worry. I've seen it before in places like this. They usually leave the whites alone.'

We talked a little more, and then five men, all in dark glasses, walked across the room to our table. One of them spoke quietly to Swanepoel. The South African pilot finished his beer quickly and left with the men.

While I was having breakfast the next morning in the hotel dining room, the waiters crowded around the radio. They were listening to the news:

'The Ugandan army has this day decided that Idi Amin Dada will be our new president. Everybody must continue their work in their usual way. Foreign governments must stay out of our country. If they send soldiers, we will fight them. Our new president will speak to us all very soon.'

Nervously, I picked up my coffee and went to the window. At first, the street seemed calm – I saw nothing unusual. Then, suddenly, it was filled with crowds of people screaming the name of Idi Amin. Groups of young men pulled pictures of Obote, the last president, down from walls.

'Obote is dead!' they shouted. (Not true, I discovered later. He was in Kenya and later moved to Tanzania.)

I decided to go down into the crowd. I had to see the Ugandan Minister of Health. I thought I should also visit the British Embassy.

'I'm sorry,' the Minister's secretary told me. 'Mr Wasswa is away. He was on the plane with President – er – *Mr* Obote. We do not know if he will come back.'

'What should I do?' I asked her. 'I have to be in Mbarara tomorrow. How do I get there?'

'The bus is the best way. You must find Doctor Merrit. This

is his phone number.

I thanked her and went to the British Embassy – a big, white building. Two sunburned British soldiers on guard outside the gates checked my papers and passport. Then they sent me to a man called Nigel Stone.

'Obote is dead!' they shouted.

In his office, Stone listened carefully as I told him about myself. Then he smiled and said, 'All the trouble's been in the city. Mbarara will be safe.'

'Really?' I asked, a little surprised. 'So I should go there?'

'Of course. I think things will calm down very quickly. We're glad that Amin's going to be the new president. He fought for the British here in Africa, you know. He's not very clever, but he won't give us any trouble.'

He wrote down my parents' names and my home address in a big brown book. Then he asked me, 'How are you planning to get to Mbarara?'

'By bus.'

'Buses here are very dangerous vehicles.' He shook his head sadly. 'I'm sorry we don't have an embassy car for you. Ah, well, don't worry. I'm sure you'll be all right.' He closed his book and I stood up. 'Doctor Garrigan,' Stone said, and I sat down again. 'We − er − we need British people outside the cities to keep their eyes and ears open.'

'Do you want me to be a spy?' I asked, very surprised.

'No, no, but tell us if you hear anything unusual or interesting. The next time you're in Kampala, visit me.'

♦

The bus for Mbarara was old and dirty with broken windows. It was built for ten passengers, but inside there were about thirty people with a large number of farm animals. As I took my seat at the back, everyone looked at me with amused interest. I was the only white person on the bus. I smiled back at them shyly.

During the journey, I had a conversation with a friendly young man sitting next to me.

'I'm a student of Food Science at Makerere University in Kampala,' he told me. 'And you?'

'I'm a doctor.'

'You will be at the clinic with Doctor Merrit?' he asked.

'That's right.'

'I'm glad you are coming. We need good doctors – if they are not too expensive! My name is Boniface Malumba, but you must call me Bonney. I am visiting my family in Mbarara. You are welcome at my father's house. I will send for you.'

After a long, tiring journey, we arrived in Mbarara late that afternoon. I stayed with Doctor Merrit and his wife, Joyce, for one night. The following morning, after a wonderful breakfast, Merrit took me to my bungalow. Inside it was light and airy, with simple wooden furniture, whitewashed walls and – strangest of all – a stone bath. I looked through the dirty glass of the window at the green valley and the mountains.

'It's a beautiful view,' I said.

'They call it the Bachwezi Valley,' Merrit told me. 'Not much grows there. The ground's too wet.'

We went back outside into the early morning sun and climbed up a hill towards the clinic.

The clinic was a circle of simple, low buildings. A long line of women with screaming babies, sick old men and a few badly wounded soldiers waited outside its main door. Merrit showed me around the different buildings before taking me into a large room full of beds and sick people.

'Hello, everybody,' he said loudly. 'This is Doctor Garrigan. He's joining our team here.'

He then introduced me to all the nurses and nursing assistants. At one bed, a young white woman with dark brown hair was taking a sick man's temperature.

'This is Sara Zach,' Merrit told me. 'She's here with us from the University of Tel Aviv.'

'Hello,' said Sara Zach, looking at me over her shoulder. 'Welcome to our clinic.' She gave me a friendly smile, then continued with her work.

At the end of the day, I stood outside under the stars, listened to the sounds of the animals and looked out over the valley. This was my home now – and I felt wonderful.

◆

During the day, I worked hard in the clinic. In the evening, I sat outside my bungalow and wrote my thoughts and memories of the day in my notebook.

On my way to work one morning, I met Sara. We stopped half way up the hill to the clinic and looked down at some army buildings near the town. There was a lot of activity that morning. Officers were shouting orders and the men were running up and down busily.

'A lot of soldiers are leaving to fight this afternoon,' Sara said seriously. 'Let's go. We'll be late for work.'

During the following week, a large number of people came to the clinic for help.

'I was knifed,' many of them reported. Others said, 'Soldiers shot me.'

'Why?' I asked Sara.

'Obote's rebels are hiding across the border in Rwanda,' she explained. 'Amin's men are punishing the local people for helping them. The lucky ones are brought here. Others are less lucky. They're dead.'

For the next few weeks, I took medicine out to the villages around Mbarara. I travelled with a friendly, white-haired African called William Waziri.

On our return to Mbarara, we were stopped outside the town by soldiers. They pushed guns through the windows of our Land Rover and shouted something at William. When he didn't answer, they became angrier. I was beginning to feel frightened. Then William threw some money at them and they let us past.

To calm ourselves, we went for a drink in the Changalulu,

one of the bars in town. We drank a lot and stayed very late. Finally, there was only one other customer in the bar. I saw from his uniform that he was an important army officer. He was looking unhappily into his glass. Finally, he stood up, gave us a long hard look, and walked slowly out of the bar.

'That's Major Mabuse,' William told me. 'He was a taxi driver when Obote was president. A very unpleasant man.'

'They all seem unpleasant to me.'

'But Amin is the most unpleasant of them all. He's a terrible man. He's coming here next month to make a speech.'

'Will you go?' I asked him.

'Of course not,' he replied. 'I hate him.'

♦

One Sunday, the Malumba family invited me to lunch. Boniface greeted me at the door.

'My long-lost friend, Doctor Nicholas!'

Mrs Malumba, a short fat woman in a long dress, offered to wash my feet. I refused, of course. It was quite a modern house, compared with other local houses. They even had a black-and-white television.

The father was fat too, but tall and proud-looking. He was sitting in an armchair when I came in, with a glass of beer in his hand. Gugu, Bonney's younger brother, was playing on the floor. Bonney introduced me to his father, and I sat down in an armchair. After a few minutes' polite conversation, the subject soon turned to the political situation. It was clear that Mr Malumba didn't like Idi Amin.

'I went to Kampala a short time ago,' he said. 'Amin has filled the army and police with all his friends from the north. They're different from us. They're no better than criminals.'

'They are still people, Father,' Bonney said. 'It doesn't matter which part of the country people come from.'

There followed a noisy, angry conversation between Mr Malumba and his son. Mrs Malumba smiled and went to the kitchen. Gugu picked up his toys and ran outside. Finally, Mr Malumba shook his head and went for a sleep.

After lunch, Bonney and I watched an old English-language film on TV. Walking back to my bungalow, I thought about the film. For the first time since my arrival in Uganda, I thought about my home in Scotland and I felt sad.

♦

A few days later, the President arrived in Mbarara to make a speech at the football ground. I was in the crowd with Sara to hear him.

As he stepped up onto the stage, the crowd danced and screamed with great excitement. Sara held my arm tightly as people pushed around us.

'I'm surprised at his popularity,' she said.

At last, the crowd calmed down and Amin spoke into the microphone. 'I have come to talk to you about God,' he said. 'God has made you, the people of Mbarara, the best people in Uganda. Yes, I am very proud of you.'

Again, the crowd went crazy.

'But,' Amin continued, 'better worlds than this are possible. It doesn't matter if you are Christian or Muslim. You will make a better world if you believe in God very strongly. You cannot see him, but he is there.'

'He's a very deep thinker, isn't he?' I joked to Sara.

But Sara didn't hear me. She was listening carefully to the speech and writing notes in a small notebook.

Amin continued to shout into the microphone. 'I am the most powerful person in Uganda. But I am also only an ordinary Ugandan. I know everything in all your hearts. I live inside each of you. I know your hopes and your dreams.'

Suddenly, I discovered that I too was listening to his words with great interest. His message was strange – crazy even – but his voice was mysteriously powerful. The crowd loved him. I could understand why.

Sara held my arm tightly as people pushed around us.

'We must work together,' he shouted. 'If we do not, we will be under the power of the white man again. There are bad people and spies living secretly in our country. They want to give back power to the white man. We must find them and throw them out immediately. If we do not, there will be great sickness in our land.'

Sara looked around nervously. 'We need to go,' she said quietly. 'It's possible that they will attack us.'

'Don't be silly,' I smiled.

But I could tell from the worried look on her face that she wasn't joking.

We pushed our way through the crowd and out of the football ground. In silence, we climbed the long, steep road out of town. Finally, we were standing outside my bungalow.

'Would you like to come in for a coffee,' I asked her.

'I have work to do,' she replied.

'But it's Saturday.'

'Sorry,' she said, looking at me strangely. 'Maybe another time.'

Chapter 3 Sara

Time passed very quickly, and I was soon in my second year in Uganda. Sara and I were becoming friendlier and friendlier while, at the same time, the area was becoming more and more dangerous. One night, I heard the sound of shooting and explosions in Mbarara. I stood outside my bungalow and watched the fires down below. I asked William Waziri about it the next morning.

'Major Mabuse's men have killed all the local soldiers here,' he told me. He looked tired. 'I saw lorries taking the bodies away into the forest. It was sickening.'

The next day, two Americans arrived in Mbarara in a blue

Volkswagen. They started asking questions about the soldiers. A few days later, they both disappeared. I didn't know them, but Sara did.

'I met one of them a few days ago,' she said. 'He was a newspaper reporter, he said. He wanted information about the killings.'

'The Americans had a problem with Major Mabuse,' William explained to me later. 'People say that his soldiers killed them. Their bodies were left, covered in earth, by the side of the road.'

The next day, I saw Major Mabuse in town. He was driving a blue Volkswagen.

◆

One Sunday in June, Sara and I drove up to a lake in the mountains. It was beautiful. Sara's head was on my chest. The hills were a deep green and the lake shone like silver. The sky was filled with brightly coloured birds.

Suddenly, we heard a strange sound coming from the valley below us – the sound of Scottish music! Looking down, we saw a large group of Ugandan soldiers dressed in Scottish uniforms. We watched them in silence as they walked past us and down the narrow path towards the town. We couldn't believe our eyes.

The next morning, I woke up in Sara's house and heard the sound of her voice in the next room. She was talking urgently into the radio.

'Who were you talking to?' I asked her later.

'Tel Aviv. They're not paying me enough money.'

'I need more money too,' I smiled. But Sara didn't seem amused. 'What's the matter?' I asked her.

'Nothing,' she replied.

◆

Later that year, I went on another tour of the local villages, but this time without William. He was on holiday.

Everything was fine until I got back. When I arrived home that evening, I found a child in my doorway. It was Gugu, Bonney Malumba's little brother. He looked pale and frightened.

'What's the matter?' I asked him.

He didn't reply, but pointed down the hill towards a big cloud of black smoke over the town. I could see that something terrible was happening. I left Gugu safely in my bungalow and ran down the hill into Mbarara. Crowds of people were in the street where the Malumbas lived. They were shouting: '*Amin daima!*' Amin for ever.

Part of the street was on fire, and about twenty or thirty bodies lay outside the houses. In the middle of the crowd, I noticed Merrit on his knees, helping a badly wounded young woman. His wife and Sara were standing behind him.

'Nicholas!' Sara cried, reaching for my arm. 'We were worried about you.'

'Why?'

'Haven't you heard?' Merrit asked. 'Obote's rebels crossed the border today. About a thousand of them. They attacked the town. We've been busy here all day.'

Sara took my arm. 'Nicholas,' she said softly. 'I'm sorry. Your friend is dead.'

'What friend?' I said.

She took me to the line of bodies in the street and pointed to one of them. I didn't know who it was at first. The face was covered in blood. But then I saw the bodies on either side: Mr and Mrs Malumba, both of them dead. There was a big hole in Mr Malumba's stomach.

I turned away and started shaking. Sara held my shoulders tightly. Not far away from me, four men lifted a body into the back of a lorry. They held it by its arms and legs. It was Bonney.

Somewhere behind me, through my sadness and pain, I heard the voices of two women talking slowly and carefully, like two actors in a theatre.

'Is the lake calm?'

'No, the lake is not calm.'

'Is God watching us?'

'No, God is not watching.'

♦

Gugu stayed with us for a short time. Sara and I didn't know what to do with him. We tried everything – games, stories, jokes – but he never spoke a single word.

A month later, Gugu's uncle came to the bungalow. He wanted to take Gugu away to live with his family. Sara and I watched the little boy quietly as he was taken away.

'We can't do anything more,' she said sadly. Then she turned and looked at me, her brown eyes full of pain. 'You should leave Uganda soon, Nicholas. Things will go badly here.'

'What do you mean?' I said, following her back into the house. 'How do you know?'

'It's like in Israel. You *feel* when there will be trouble.'

I put my arm around her, but she moved away from me.

After that, Sara began to act differently towards me. She spent fewer nights with me and spoke to me less often in the clinic. When I visited in the evening, her bungalow was often empty.

She spent a lot of time in Mbarara with a team of Israeli road builders who were working on a new road to Fort Portal, near the border with Zaire. One night, I followed her into town and found her in a bar. She was with the road builders. They were all standing over a map on the table and talking quickly in Hebrew. She saw me, but didn't say hello. I drank a glass of beer and left.

At midnight she came to my bungalow and was angry with

me. 'Stop following me!' she shouted. 'They are *my* people. It's *my* business what I do with them!'

Things began to go badly at the clinic too. William Waziri didn't come back after his holiday. Merrit was very angry – not only about William, but about everything. There was less and less money for medicines, and the news on the radio about Idi Amin was becoming stranger and stranger. One day, the BBC reported a message from Amin to the Queen of England:

'Scotland must be free,' the message said. 'The Scots will fight if the English do not leave their country. Many Scottish people say that I am the last King of the Scots. I will gladly be their king.'

On Ugandan radio, Amin made another speech: 'Indians came to Uganda to build the railway,' he said. 'The railway is finished. They must leave now.'

The next day in town, I saw a group of Indian shopkeepers in the street. Soldiers were cutting their faces with broken bottles. A short time later, their shops and businesses were taken away by Major Mabuse. He gave their shops to Ugandan army officers. Prices went up and businesses soon failed. It became impossible to buy milk, salt, soap or sugar. In the end, 50,000 Indians were sent out of the country, the BBC said, without a penny in their pockets.

One day, Sara didn't come to work at the clinic. When I went to her bungalow at lunchtime, the door was unlocked. I went inside. Her things were gone.

I felt angry with her. 'Why didn't she say goodbye?' I asked myself. But I knew why. She didn't want me to stop her going.

Later, Merrit's servant explained how she left. 'The Israeli road builders took her away in their Land Rover early this morning,' he said. 'They escaped over the mountain to Rwanda. All Israelis have to leave the country in the next three days. Those are Amin's orders.'

I was now deeply unhappy in Mbarara. My life there seemed empty without Sara. Then Idi Amin's car accident on a narrow country road changed my life completely. After some thought, I accepted the offer to become his personal doctor in Kampala. I could leave Mbarara and my memories of Sara behind.

Chapter 4   A Lazy Life

In Kampala, I didn't see Amin for a long time. He was too busy for doctors, it seemed. I was given a bungalow at the President's main home, State House, but for three days a week I worked at Mulago, the biggest hospital in Kampala. People from many different countries worked there. I thought about doing some serious study into African illnesses. But I did nothing in the end because I was too lazy.

In my free time I shopped, ate in good restaurants and swam in the pool of one of the city's big hotels. It was at this swimming pool that I became friendly with Marina Perkins, the British ambassador's beautiful young wife. She asked me about my life in Mbarara and I asked her about life in Kampala.

'It's boring,' she said. 'I've done everything interesting already. But I haven't been fishing on Lake Victoria yet. I've asked my husband to take me. But he's always busy and he doesn't like water.'

About a month after my arrival in Kampala, I received a phone call. This was the first of many similar calls.

'Hello, hello, Doctor. President Amin here. Come now to my house. My son is very, very sick. You must drive here immediately. I am in Prince Charles Drive.'

'But I don't have a car.'

'Tell the soldiers at the gate outside your bungalow to bring you. Immediately!'

Twenty minutes later, one of Amin's wives greeted me at the door of an ordinary-looking house in Prince Charles Drive.

'I am sorry, Doctor,' she said. 'The President has gone away on urgent government business. My name is Kay. I am the boy's mother.'

I followed her inside the house. The living room floor was covered with plastic toys. Children ran around shouting and crying. There was a smell of cooking from the kitchen, and everything seemed very ordinary.

Upstairs, in a bedroom, a ten-year-old boy was lying in bed. He was in pain, and blood was coming out of his nose.

'Is it bad, Doctor?' asked his mother nervously.

I shone a small light up the boy's nose. 'Oh, no,' I smiled. 'Nothing serious. He's pushed something up there.'

Kay Amin held the boy down while I slowly and carefully pulled something small and hard out of his nose. I cleaned it and held it up to the light. It was a small plastic toy soldier.

'Campbell,' she said angrily to her son. 'You're a very bad boy.'

I cleaned the boy's nose. 'He'll be fine,' I said.

Kay Amin walked me to the door. 'Thank you very much, Doctor,' she said. 'The President will be very pleased.'

The following week, I found a Toyota outside my bungalow. There was an envelope on the driver's seat and, inside it, there was a message from Wasswa on government paper:

'The President is very grateful to you for making his son better,' the Health Minister wrote. 'He has given you this car to say thank you for your help.'

I was very happy. With a car, I could now drive myself around the city. Life became a lot more fun.

♦

One Friday night I went to a bar called the Stratocruise with Peter Mbalu-Mukasa, one of the African doctors at Mulago.

There, we met Freddy Swanepoel, the South African pilot. Swanepoel was soon joking about Amin in a very loud voice.

'Be careful,' Peter said quietly. 'Someone will report you.'

'He won't hurt me,' Swanepoel said. 'I'm too useful to him.'

'Everyone is useful to him – for a short time,' Peter replied. 'He has even killed some army officers who helped him against Obote. His soldiers will attack the white people soon.'

'No they won't,' said Swanepoel. 'Amin needs us.'

'I was talking to the British Ambassador's wife a few days ago,' I said. 'She agrees with Swanepoel. She doesn't think that whites are in danger.'

'Marina Perkins?' Swanepoel said, touching his beard with a thoughtful look on his face. 'What does *she* know? I met her once or twice. She's a nice woman, but she doesn't understand the political situation.'

'Exactly,' Peter said. '*Nobody* understands the political situation. Not even Amin. I know this. I know people who work very closely with him.'

'Who?' Swanepoel wanted to know.

'I can't say.' Peter looked nervous suddenly.

Swanepoel smiled and shook his head. 'You mustn't show people like Amin that you're afraid. If you do, they'll destroy you. They're like dogs. They can smell fear.'

'You don't understand,' Peter said. 'He's destroying us already. The soldiers have attacked students at the university.'

'Don't worry,' Swanepoel said. 'Someone will destroy *him* soon. People like him only stay in power for a short time.'

A week later, Amin telephoned me at the hospital.

'Hello, hello, it's Doctor Idi Amin here,' he said. 'I am very pleased with my doctors at Mulago. I would like you and Doctor Paterson to join me for lunch tomorrow at Cape Town, one o'clock.' Paterson also worked at the hospital.

The line went dead before I could reply.

Everyone knew about 'Cape Town'. It was the name of Amin's new house on Lake Victoria. He now had four houses in the Kampala–Entebbe area: State House, Prince Charles Drive, Nakasero Lodge and Cape Town.

'I know why he's invited us,' Paterson said. 'He wants to hear us being rude about the English.'

'Why?'

'Because we're Scottish. He thinks that all Scots hate the English. We must talk about other things.'

'Like what?'

'The importance of seat belts on Ugandan roads is a good subject.'

The next afternoon, Paterson and I discussed seat belts with Idi Amin in the garden of his new house by Lake Victoria. But the conversation soon turned to the political situation.

'You see, it's very true,' Amin said. 'Scotland and Uganda have both suffered greatly because of the English. That is why I am going to make war on British businesses in Uganda. What do you think?'

Paterson tried to talk about seat belts again. 'I really think there are too many road accidents in Uganda, Mr President,' he said.

Amin looked at him strangely. 'Why do you always talk to me about seat belts, Doctor Paterson? Every time we meet, you talk about seat belts! There are more urgent problems in Uganda than that!' He stood up quickly. 'Now you must go,' he said. 'You have made me angry with this talk of seat belts.'

'Perhaps,' Paterson said on the way back, 'the subject of seat belts wasn't a great idea.'

The next morning on the radio, I listened to the BBC news. Someone from the British government was talking about Idi Amin's plans to attack British businesses in Uganda. As I listened, I made myself a cup of coffee. Suddenly, I remembered my early-morning cups of coffee in Mbarara with Sara, and a feeling of sadness came over me.

'Why hasn't she written?' I asked myself. 'Why hasn't she called?'

Chapter 5 'The Craziest Man in Africa!'

The following week, Nigel Stone called me to the British Embassy. Bob Perkins, the ambassador, and another man, Major Weir, were also waiting for me in his office when I arrived. Perkins greeted me with a friendly smile and offered me a seat. He then sat next to Stone on the opposite side of the table. Weir stood quietly behind them, smoking a cigarette.

'Amin's acting very strangely,' Perkins said.

'We need your help,' Stone added. 'You promised to help us in Mbarara. Do you remember?'

'Yes. I'm sorry I didn't do anything,' I replied.

'Oh, that doesn't matter,' Perkins said. 'But we really do need your help now. Amin's army is killing a lot of people.'

'You've seen the bodies,' Stone added urgently.

'But I'm only a doctor,' I said. 'What can *I* do?'

'As his personal doctor,' Perkins suggested, 'you can talk to him. The killing has to stop. He's also planning to throw British businessmen out of the country. Tell him why it's a bad idea. He will listen to you.'

'And if he doesn't?'

'Give him some strong medicine that will calm him down,' Stone said.

I looked up at Weir. He was watching me coldly, almost angrily, like a head teacher looking at a bad pupil.

'I can't do that,' I said at last. 'It's unprofessional.'

'I disagree,' said Stone. 'As a doctor, you have to make him well. Stop him acting in this crazy, dangerous way.'

Weir gave me a small, strange smile. His eyes shone with secret amusement. I felt suddenly ill. The smell of his smoke was making me very light-headed. Stone and Perkins continued talking. They gave me more reasons and they made a lot of suggestions. In the end I didn't say yes or no.

'I'll think about it,' I said.

Perkins was right. During the next few days, Amin started to make life very difficult for British people in Uganda. He ordered a lot of them out of the country immediately. One of them was Merrit. He came to see me on his way to the airport.

'You're clearly Amin's favourite son,' he said coldly.

He looked unwell – thin and pale. He was still angry with me for leaving the clinic so suddenly.

'I was the last white person there in the end,' he said.

♦

One day, I nervously invited Marina Perkins to go fishing with me on Lake Victoria. Surprisingly, she accepted my invitation.

A few days later, we were alone together on a small boat in the middle of the lake.

I told Marina about Merrit leaving the country. She wasn't surprised.

'It's not only him, you know,' she said. 'My husband thinks *we'll* have to leave soon too.'

I said nothing about the conversation with her husband and Stone at the Embassy.

'Strange things are happening,' she continued. 'A few days ago, Weir was suddenly sent back to Scotland. He was getting too friendly with Amin, my husband said. He was helping Amin with plans for an attack on Tanzania. I always thought Weir was a strange man. But I must stop talking about it. Bob has told me never to discuss his work with other people

... Look at those birds.' She pointed behind me. 'Aren't they beautiful?'

A short time later, I found a quiet place near an island and stopped the boat. I picked up some fishing equipment. 'Let's try here,' I suggested.

I threw the line into the water and waited. There were no bites. I tried again, but still had no success.

'Would *you* like to try?' I asked Marina.

*A few days later, we were alone together on a small boat
in the middle of the lake.*

'Why not?' she smiled. 'But I don't know how to throw a line.'

I stood behind her and, with my hand on her wrist, showed her how. We stood there silently in the boat under beautiful African clouds of pink and red. The only noise was the sound of water against the side of the boat. I could feel the heat of her body through her thin summer dress. Suddenly, I lowered my head and kissed her arm. Marina jumped. The fishing equipment fell from her hand.

'What are you doing?' she shouted

'I ... I ...' I didn't know what to say.

'Take me back now,' she said. 'Immediately. Have you forgotten? I'm the wife of the British Ambassador!'

'I'm sorry,' I said quietly. 'That was stupid of me.'

I piloted the boat away from the island and we sailed back in silence.

♦

A week after the boat trip, Wasswa called me at the hospital.

'Come quickly,' he said. 'The President is sick. He is at Nakasero.'

'At last,' I thought, 'I can do the job that I'm paid for.'

Wasswa was waiting for me when I arrived. 'He has a pain in his stomach,' he explained.

Amin was lying face down on his bed when we entered the bedroom. There were clothes, magazines and sports equipment all over the floor. Wasswa left the room and I began my examination.

Amin was like a big baby. He thought he was dying. But the pain was only the result of too much food. I pressed down hard on his stomach. There was a loud, unpleasant noise, and air came out. Amin suddenly smiled.

'You are a very clever man,' he said. 'You have saved my life. Now we will go for a drink!'

A few hours later, I drove Amin back to State House. It was late, but he wasn't tired. He wanted to sit and talk. As he talked about his love for the Queen of England but his hate for English people, I thought about Stone's request for my help. Perhaps now was a good time to talk to Amin.

'Your army kills a lot of people. Why don't you stop them?' I suggested nervously.

Amin shook his head sadly. 'Doctor Nicholas, sometimes you must kill to give other people a better life. That is the situation in the world today. This I know.'

I said nothing more about the killings.

♦

Life continued. I went to work. I ate. I slept. I got older. Sometimes I thought about Stone's request, but only when Amin was ill. In all my six years in Kampala, he wasn't ill very often. Amin offered me a house on Lake Victoria, but I stayed in the bungalow at State House. Sometimes Amin invited me to his house at Nakasero for tea.

One day, his enemies tried to kill him. He was leaving the Nsambya Police Sports Ground when someone in the crowd shot at his Land Rover. Luckily for Amin, the gunman hit his driver, not him. That night, Kampala was filled with soldiers and many people in the city were killed as punishment for the attack.

'I was saved by God,' Amin told me later. 'I will not die until God is ready for me. I know it.'

As the months passed, Amin became stranger and stranger. For one conversation with foreign reporters, for example, he wore orange sports clothes. He joked with them as they asked him questions. Then a woman asked him about the killing of people by his soldiers. He stood up and walked towards her angrily. 'You people are very bad,' he said. 'You ask me so many questions. How much do you need to know? Be careful.

No one can run faster than a gun can shoot.'

The following day, there was a picture of him on the front page of a newspaper in England. Above it, in big letters, were the words 'The Craziest Man in Africa!'

While Amin became stranger, he also became friendlier. He telephoned me all the time. He wrote letters to kings and presidents around the world, and he often proudly showed them to me. I remember one letter to Margaret Thatcher.

'What do you think of this?' he asked. Then he read it to me:

'Dear Margaret, I saw your picture in an East African newspaper on Tuesday. You were laughing. In the photograph, you look strong, happy and intelligent. I hope you have a happy life. Your friend, Idi Amin.'

'Don't send it,' I told him.

'Oh, I *will* send it,' he said. 'It is very important.'

Some letters were amusing. For example, to President Julius Nyerere of Tanzania, after a disagreement, he wrote:

'I want to tell you that I love you. I would like to marry you. But, sadly, because you are a man, I cannot.'

'Why do you send these letters?' I asked him.

'It is simple,' Amin replied. 'I like to be honest with people. When people do something wrong, I tell them. When they are right, I tell them that too. I am a messenger from God.'

Some of his letters were not funny. For example, he wrote to the head of the West German government, Willy Brandt:

'Hitler was right about the Jews because the Israelis are only interested in war. That is why Israelis were gassed in Germany.'

I heard Willy Brandt speak on BBC radio the following day.

'Idi Amin has a sick mind,' he said. 'He needs help.'

Of course, I agreed with him. I could see that Amin was dangerous and crazy. But I couldn't leave. This terrible man had a strange, mysterious power over me. To me, he was more interesting than frightening. That is why I stayed.

Then, one month, everything seemed to go wrong for me.

Chapter 6 'I'm Not a Killer'

One night, during a bad storm, there was a knock at the door of my bungalow. It was Peter Mbalu-Mukasa, from the hospital. He looked terrible, shaking with cold in the heavy rain.

'Come in,' I said. 'What's the matter?'

At first, he didn't say anything. He sat shaking on a chair in front of me. Finally, he lifted his head and began to speak.

'For almost a year, Kay Amin has been my lover,' he said quietly. 'It is unwise, I know. But we are very much in love.'

'My God,' I said. 'But you've got a wife.'

'We have a big problem,' Peter continued. 'Kay is going to have a baby. Amin hasn't slept with her for years. If he discovers this, he will kill us both. She must have an abortion. I need your help.'

'I can't do that,' I said. 'You should both leave the country. You'll reach the Tanzanian border by morning if you leave now.'

'I thought of that, but escape is impossible. All the police and soldiers know Kay's face. They are sure to stop us at the border, if not before. Kay has asked for you. We have to go now.'

Feeling very unhappy about it, I drove him in my car to a small flat in Kampala. Kay was lying on a sheet on the living-room floor. I looked down at the poor woman. She was clearly feeling very afraid and nervous. She was looking around the room, her hands on her stomach, talking crazily to herself.

'This isn't possible,' I said to Peter. 'I've never done an abortion before.'

He held my arm tightly. 'Nicholas … please.'

'It's not right. You must try to escape. Or take her to

27

Mulago. They have better equipment there.'

'Don't be stupid. This is the only way.' He pulled me close to him. 'Please,' he said urgently. 'I'm not sure I can do it.'

The room fell silent except for Kay's soft, frightened voice. I wanted to help them. But finally, I decided that I couldn't.

'I have to leave now,' I said. 'Please, Peter, don't do this. You can solve this problem in another way. I will help you if I can. Ring me.'

I turned and left the room.

Was I right not to help them? I still don't know. But after that night, I never saw Peter Mbalu-Mukasa or Kay Amin again. Peter didn't listen to me. He did the abortion, but it went wrong. Kay lost too much blood and died. The next day, Peter killed himself.

The following week, Amin called me, his three other wives, twenty children and other politicians to see Kay's body at Mulago hospital.

As he spoke, many of the children were crying. The wives looked frightened and the politicians looked serious.

'This was a bad woman,' Amin said. 'She coloured her face, arms and legs to look white. The other parts of her body stayed black. See how unnatural she looks. Her death is the judgement of God.'

♦

One evening later that month, I went for a walk in a park near the city centre. From the path, I had a clear view of lighted tables near the bar of the Imperial Hotel. At one table I saw a man and a woman. He was wearing a coffee-coloured shirt and short trousers. She was wearing a summer dress. They were laughing together. Then the man's hand moved to the woman's knee.

The man was Freddy Swanepoel and the woman was Marina Perkins.

That night, I felt very unhappy. I drank beer until I was completely drunk. 'What's wrong with me?' I thought. 'Why is Marina happy when Swanepoel touches her? Why was she so angry with me when I kissed her on the arm?'

I felt terrible all week – not just because of Swanepoel and Marina. I thought of all the bad things in my life: Sara's disappearance, Stone's request, Kay's abortion, the strangeness of Amin ... and perhaps, most of all, the fact that I was still in Uganda. I was still Amin's doctor.

Even Amin noticed that something was wrong.

'What's the matter?' he asked when I next saw him.

I told him everything about Swanepoel and Marina. He put a hand on my shoulder and looked into my eyes.

'Don't be sad,' he said warmly. 'That man is the best pilot in Africa – except for me – but he is no good. Don't worry about him. It is bad to play around with other people's wives. It is also bad to spy on President Amin. He is a spy and he works for a bad Kenyan company. They are too expensive. And they never want me to pay them in Ugandan money. They only want US dollars.' He pulled some Ugandan notes from his pocket and waved them in the air. 'Why is my face on this money if I cannot use it? It is a very bad situation,' he said.

♦

Stone was looking out of the window as he talked.

'I'm glad that we're alone this time.'

'But why isn't the Ambassador here?' I asked him. 'If you're going to talk to me about the same subject as last time, I want to see the boss.'

'He's not really my boss,' Stone said carefully. 'Bob Perkins doesn't know everything about my work.'

'What happened to Weir?' I asked. 'I heard that he was sent back to London.'

'He talked too much.'

'He didn't say a word when *I* last saw him.'

Stone wasn't amused. 'About our plans,' he said. 'What have you done about Amin?'

'Nothing.'

Stone sat back in his chair thoughtfully. 'We stopped lending his country money when he threw all the Indians out. But that wasn't enough. Now there's no law and order in the country. People are disappearing every day. His soldiers are killing hundreds of people. They're putting all the bodies in the lake or hiding them in the forests. He's like Hitler.'

Stone was beginning to make me angry. 'No one's like Hitler,' I said.

He took a big envelope from his desk and gave it to me. Inside the envelope, there were photographs – terrible photographs – of killings. In one photograph, Amin was talking in a friendly way to a man with a bag over his head. In the next photograph, the same man was dead, lying in a pool of blood.

'These photographs show only a small part of the picture. We're hearing unbelievable things about him.'

I pushed the photographs back to him and said, 'I didn't know it was as bad as this.'

Stone stood up and looked down at me angrily. 'Hundreds of people are dying every day, but what are *you* doing? Worse than nothing! You're even working *with* him!'

I felt very uncomfortable. 'I don't … work *with* him. I'm his doctor, that's all. *I'm* not killing people. There are hundreds of Ugandans in the same position as me.'

'You're in a perfect position to help them and their country. You can get the right medicines – dangerous medicines. No one will ask any questions. I'm going to be honest with you. I have orders from London. They want Amin dead. I'm asking you to kill him.'

'Impossible,' I laughed. 'My job is to *save* lives, not take them.'

'If you kill this crazy man, you *will* save lives. Thousands of them.'

'Impossible,' I repeated.

'You won't be in any danger,' Stone continued. 'You can give him something and it will look like a heart attack. No one will think it was you.'

I stood up without a word and walked to the door.

'We've already paid £50,000 into your bank in Scotland.'

'I don't want your blood money.'

'You will. We'll give you another £50,000 when you've killed Amin.'

'I refuse,' I said loudly, my hand on the door. But secretly I knew that Stone was right. Amin *was* dangerous and crazy. And I *could* kill him easily. But … something in me still *liked* the man.

'Think about it seriously,' Stone said. 'We'll give you anything you want.'

'I'm not a killer,' I said.

With those words I left Stone's office.

Chapter 7 'Why Are You My Enemy?'

The following week, one of my problems was solved. Stone was told to leave the country by Amin – with Marina, her husband and all the other people at the British Embassy.

'I have sent home the British spies,' Amin said on the radio. Strangely, he also talked about his love for the Queen. 'I said to the Queen of England, "I am going to visit you soon. Yes, Mrs Queen, I am coming to London and no one can stop me.

31

I am bringing two hundred and fifty Ugandan soldiers with me. I want the British people to see the most powerful man in Africa. And I want Scotland to be free!"'

A short time after everyone from the embassy was sent home, my personal notebook was stolen from the desk in my bungalow. I was frightened because no other things were taken. Early the next evening, I received a telephone call at Mulago from Amin.

'Come to Nakasero immediately,' he said. 'I have urgent business to discuss with you. Very urgent.'

The line went dead.

During my drive to Nakasero, I felt very frightened. 'What does he know about my conversations with Stone?' I thought. 'Does he know that I saw Kay the evening before she died? Has he read my secret thoughts about him in my notebook?'

Amin was wearing an ordinary soldier's uniform when I arrived. He was sitting in the armchair next to his large, untidy bed. The floor, as usual, was covered with sports equipment, children's toys and magazines. The *Sunday Times* newspaper was lying open at his feet.

He looked up and smiled pleasantly.

'Ah,' he said. 'My good Doctor Nicholas.' He looked down at the newspaper. 'THE AFRICAN MURDERER,' he read. He lifted his eyes to me. 'The English hate me,' he said. 'But I still love the Queen. I am thinking of writing to her again.'

'Is that why you want to see me?' I was still shaking with fear.

'Yes,' he said, standing up. 'And also no. I want to talk to you about another subject. Why are you my enemy?'

I looked at him but said nothing.

'Doctor, you have started to fight against me. Like an Englishman, not a Scot. Very bad.' He put his hand in his pocket and pulled out a gun. 'This is your last day,' he said. He pointed the gun at me. 'You are going to die. This is your end.'

I went down on my knees and began to cry. 'Please, I haven't done anything wrong!'

He went down on his knees next to me and spoke softly, like a child. 'Why don't you love me?' he said. 'Why have you stopped being my friend?'

'Please don't kill me!' I said, shaking terribly.

Suddenly, he stood up and laughed loudly.

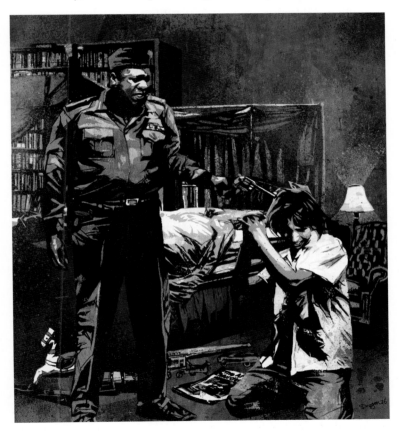

He pointed the gun at me. 'You are going to die.'

'Kill you?' he said. 'I don't want to kill you.' He put the gun in his pocket and walked across to a large mirror on the wall. 'I am sorry I frightened you,' he said. 'But I have heard bad reports about you.' He turned and waved a pink sheet of paper at me. 'This report was written by my good friend Major Weir. Sadly, he has gone now. The British government has told you to kill me. You cannot tell me that this is untrue. I know everything, you see. But I also know that you love Idi Amin too much. You don't want to hurt him.'

'That's true,' I said, still on my knees.

'So,' he said, a strange look in his eyes, 'they *did* ask you?'

'But I refused to help them. It's not right.'

'Good,' he said. He walked across the room to his desk and sat down. 'Because now I can forgive you for this.'

He held up my stolen notebook.

I looked up at him, my heart full of fear. There was silence as he slowly turned the pages. 'Have I written anything dangerous in that book?' I asked myself. But I couldn't remember. I was frightened and couldn't think clearly.

'You are a very good writer,' he finally said. 'But why have you written down our private conversations?'

'It's only a personal notebook,' I said. 'I haven't shown it to anyone.'

'I do not like what you write here about my mother. Her name was Fanta, not Pepsi-Cola. And you write very bad things about my fourth wife. If you write more things like this, you will be dead.' Then, to my surprise, he started talking about William Waziri. 'Is he your friend?' he asked.

'I worked with him at the clinic in Mbarara.'

Amin looked at me carefully. 'He was not a good doctor. He is not my friend. If he is not *my* friend, he cannot be yours. True?'

'I don't understand.'

Amin stood up and walked around the desk.

34

'Follow me,' he said, pulling me to my feet. 'I have something very important to show you.'

He walked to the bookshelves and pushed one of them. A secret door opened. Behind it was a long, dark passageway.

'Come,' Amin said.

I followed him along the dark passageway. After a few minutes, I heard the sound of a machine, and the more frightening sound of people screaming.

We reached a large metal door. Amin pressed part of the wall and the door opened. We then moved along another passageway. There was a terrible smell, and the sound of screaming became louder.

Along one side of the passage there were a lot of small, dark rooms. In one of them, a man was lying on the floor. Two soldiers were hitting him with thick, heavy belts. In the next room I saw a man in a large metal box. He was up to his neck in water. In a third, I saw the body of a boy with two broken legs. Everywhere, there was blood.

I pressed my back against the wall of the passageway. I felt sick and I couldn't move.

Amin took my arm and pulled me hard. 'Let's go,' he said coldly. 'Don't stay here. It isn't natural. There is someone that I want you to meet. He is a friend of yours.'

At the end of the passageway there was a room full of beds. All the beds were empty except one. Around it stood a number of soldiers.

'Is this your friend?' Amin asked.

The man on the bed was William Waziri. He looked up at me, his eyes full of fear. He tried to speak, but there was a piece of rough plastic in his mouth. Blood was running down his face.

Amin pressed his hand down hard on my shoulder. 'This is a bad man,' he said. 'He was working with Obote's rebels from

Tanzania and Rwanda. You were wrong to be his friend.'

'I have done nothing,' I said quietly. I tried to move away from the bed, but the soldiers stopped me.

Amin pointed at William on the bed. In a soft, quiet voice he said to the soldiers, 'Kill him.'

One of the soldiers pulled out a knife. The others pulled William to the floor. One of them put a boot on his head. William's eyes looked straight into mine. I turned away as the soldier pulled his knife across William's neck.

I woke up on the stone floor of a small room without any windows. A single yellow light hung above me. There was dry blood on the grey stone walls.

The metal door opened with a loud noise and a soldier came in with a tin dish in his hand. He shook me roughly and shouted at me angrily.

'You dirty British,' he said. 'You come here to take our sisters. Then you sleep like animals on the floor. Get up!'

When I was on my feet, he put the tin dish on the floor. Then he left the room. I looked at the food in the dish. It was watery and grey. I felt sick.

Many hours later, the same soldier came in again. 'Take off your clothes,' he said.

After I took them off, he pushed me into a shower room. When I came out, Wasswa was standing there with a towel and some new clothes over his arm.

'Are you OK, Doctor?' the Health Minister asked. 'It was very unwise of you to write about President Amin in that way. And you must stop planning activities against Uganda with our British enemies.'

'I have done nothing wrong,' I replied.

When I was dressed, I followed Wasswa along the two passageways and through the secret doors in the bookshelves back into Amin's room. Amin was watching football on TV.

He smiled when he saw me.

'Ah, my good friend Doctor Nicholas. It is very nice to see you again, yes?'

'Yes,' I replied in a flat, tired voice.

'Now, first you must have some breakfast,' he said.

During breakfast, I answered carefully when Amin asked me questions. Secretly, I was already making plans to leave the country. I wanted to take the next plane home.

After breakfast, Amin came with me to the door. 'Go back to your bungalow,' he said warmly. 'Then you will be strong to do work tomorrow. Tomorrow, I will be busy too. There are many things happening in Uganda. Oh, and one more thing. When you get home, I want you to throw away your British passport. I want you to become Ugandan. Then I will know that you really are my friend.'

Chapter 8 Hijack at Entebbe

Early the following morning, I drove to Entebbe Airport as fast as I could. I wanted to be home in Scotland again. I was also frightened. I didn't want Amin to know about my escape from his country. And I wanted to escape before he took away my British passport.

But when I got there, the airport was closed. Soldiers were everywhere. I got out of my car and pushed my way through the crowds of watching people. Next to the walkway to an Air France aeroplane, two dark-haired Arabs and a fair-haired woman were talking to a Ugandan army officer. The woman was wearing a black skirt and was holding a machine gun.

'What happened?' I asked someone in the crowd.

'Palestinians have hijacked this plane from Tel Aviv and brought it here. They want the Israelis to free Palestinian

37

prisoners. No flights are leaving the airport.'

I walked back to my car, angry with Amin, angry with the hijackers but, most of all, angry with myself. I decided to go back to Mulago. 'I'll work as usual,' I thought.

I didn't tell Paterson or the others anything about the last twenty-four hours. 'I've been sick,' I explained.

Everyone was talking about the hijack.

Later that day, the phone rang in my office. It was Wasswa.

'The President wants you at Entebbe Airport,' he said. 'He says that the hostages must have the best doctor in Uganda.'

So I drove to the airport again. All the hostages were now off the plane and in the airport building. Two hundred and fifty of them sat around in small groups. The hijackers watched them carefully, with machine guns in their hands.

The Israelis on the passenger list, and passengers with Jewish-sounding names, were soon put into a different room from the others. We were able to give them medicine. One woman, Dora Bloch, was ill and was taken to Mulago hospital.

A short time later, Amin arrived at the airport with his fourth wife, his son, Campbell, and a lot of soldiers in short white trousers and red hats. Amin was wearing an army officer's uniform.

'Hello, my good friends.' He spoke to the hostages who were not Israeli. 'I have some good news for you. The bad dream has ended. I have talked to the Palestinians, and everybody without Israeli passports or Jewish blood can go home. There is a plane waiting outside for you. OK, OK, goodbye.'

Amin then went to speak to the Israeli and Jewish hostages. 'Welcome to my country,' he said. 'I hope your stay here will be pleasant. I will try to help you. But you cannot go home yet, I am afraid. The Palestinians are good, honest people, but the Israeli government is not being helpful about their request. So you must stay until Tel Aviv changes its mind. Please, do not try to escape. The Palestinians will shoot you if you do. I am sorry for your difficult situation. I hope Tel Aviv will give the Palestinians what they are asking for. Then nobody will have to die.'

He waved goodbye and walked out of the airport building.

◆

That night, the phone rang while I was lying in bed.

'Doctor Nicholas Garrigan?' a voice said. 'I have Major Sara Zach on the line for you from Tel Aviv.'

I thought it was a joke. 'Sara?' I said. 'Is that really you? Major? What is this?'

'It's me,' she said. 'I need to talk to you.'

'You left me,' I said. 'Why didn't you say goodbye?'

'I had to go,' she said. 'But we can't talk about that now,' she added impatiently. 'There are more important things. Have you been to the airport since the hijack?'

'Yes, but how did you know I was here in Kampala?'

'There isn't time to explain. Nicholas, I need you to do two things. First, tell me everything that you saw at the airport. Describe the airport building and the room with the hostages. How many soldiers are there? How many hijackers? How exactly is the building defended?'

I told Sara everything that I knew.

'I also want you to speak to Amin. Talk to him about the hostages. Ask him to free them.'

'I can't do that,' I said. 'Did you know I've already been in prison?'

'I'm sorry, but you must try. Please. We don't have much time.'

I didn't speak to Amin. I was too frightened. I was more interested in escaping from the country. Then, one day, government officers took away my British passport and gave me a Ugandan one in its place. How could I escape now, without a British passport and with the airport closed?

I continued to work at Mulago during the next week, with a strange feeling of emptiness inside. I understood that Sara was a spy. But did I really mean nothing to her?

During the hostage situation, life was even worse than usual.

One day, the hospital had no water. Suddenly, the toilets didn't work. We couldn't clean the floors or wash the sick people. And we didn't have enough medicine or other hospital equipment – thieves were stealing from us all the time.

The situation was bad outside the hospital too. Many of the shops were almost empty. Fruit, coffee and sugar were becoming more expensive daily. There were stories about the murder of many white people.

Then came the attack on Entebbe Airport. Israeli soldiers landed at Entebbe one night and killed all the hijackers. Most of the hostages were saved.

At Mulago, we received about fifty badly wounded Ugandan soldiers. Other soldiers came to the hospital and took Dora Bloch away. Nobody tried to stop them. We were all too afraid. Dora Bloch was never seen again.

Chapter 9 War

'Doctor Nicholas,' Amin said during our next meeting, 'I have something to show you.' A servant brought in a box and Amin opened it. 'I have a gift here for my very good friend Freddy Swanepoel.'

He pulled out something large, yellow and hairy. It was a lion's head.

'I would like you to take this to him at the airport. You know him, I believe? If you do this for me, we will forget all about your crimes against the state.'

I picked up the box. It was surprisingly heavy.

When I got to the airport, I walked past the smoke-blackened airport building to a small aeroplane on the far side of the airfield.

Swanepoel came down the steps to meet me.

'What are *you* doing here?' he shouted at me above the noise of the plane. 'Have we had to wait because of you?'

I thought of his hand on Marina Perkins's knee. I still wanted to hit him. 'I had to come,' I shouted back. 'Amin wanted me to bring you this.'

I gave him the box.

'What is it?' he said, looking down.

'It's a gift from Amin. A lion's head.'

'Stupid man,' he said. 'He wants to make sure that we continue to work for him. Last time it was a bird in a glass case.'

Minutes later, the plane was in the sky. And I was suddenly angry with myself. 'I'm so stupid,' I thought. 'Why didn't I get on that plane too?'

The following morning, I listened to the BBC. There was news of problems between Amin and President Nyerere of Tanzania. And:

'Yesterday afternoon over Kenya's Ngong Hills, there was an explosion on a small plane. Two people died – Mr Michael Roberts, the head of Rafiki, a Kenyan flying company, and the pilot, Mr Frederik Swanepoel. The reason for the explosion is unknown.'

I felt terrible. I knew immediately what happened. I wasn't the murderer, but – unknowingly – I carried death to him in the form of explosives. Why did Amin want to kill him, or his boss? Did he want to kill me too?

After Swanepoel's death, I wanted to leave the country even more urgently.

◆

While I was planning my escape, Amin's army attacked Tanzania. At the same time, I received a letter from the Merrits' old servant in Mbarara:

'Sir, I am writing to you because you were here before. The boy Gugu, Boniface Malumba's little brother, has been very bad. He is in great trouble. Please come quickly to Mbarara and help him.'

Memories of my time in Mbarara, the happiest days of my stay in Uganda, came back to me. 'Amin has done many bad things,' I thought, 'but I've done nothing about them. Now I can help one young boy. I'll drive down to Mbarara. From there, I'll escape with Gugu across the border into Rwanda.'

I made my preparations quickly and was soon driving to Mbarara. During the journey I had many frightening and unpleasant adventures. Soldiers in a Land Rover drove after me into a forest. I hid from them but they destroyed my car. In the forest I saw piles of dead bodies and the smell of them made me sick. Then I ate a dangerous plant by mistake and was very ill. My life was saved by people who lived in the forest. Days later, when I was well, I continued my journey on foot.

At last, I saw Mbarara. As I walked towards the town, I heard the sound of pop music on a radio and, more frighteningly, the sound of explosions in the hills. In front of the gates to the army buildings, I saw a small crowd of people. They were excited about something. I pushed through them and saw someone tied to a chair. Four boys in army uniform were hitting him with guns and sticks. There was the sound of another explosion, louder this time. People started to run away. I moved towards the boy on the chair. I wanted to save him. 'Perhaps it's Gugu,' I thought.

As I reached him, I looked at the face covered in blood. No, it wasn't Gugu. Then one of the boy soldiers turned and looked at me angrily. I knew his face immediately. *This* was Gugu! Before I could speak, Gugu hit me hard with his gun. I fell to the ground in great pain. Suddenly, there was another big explosion. I covered my ears and shut my eyes.

Minutes later, I opened my eyes and looked around me. I saw Gugu's face next me. His eyes were open and blood was coming out of his mouth. His headless body was lying a long way away. The top of his neck was red, like a half-opened flower.

When I woke up again, I was in the back of a moving vehicle. A hand passed me a big cup of tea and a piece of dry bread.

'Where am I?' I said.

'You are now protected by the Tanzanian army,' a friendly voice told me. 'My name is Major Kuchasa. We have just completed a successful attack against Mbarara. You are very lucky to be alive. What are you doing here?'

'I've had enough of Uganda,' I told him. 'I wanted to cross the border into Rwanda.'

'That isn't possible now,' Major Kuchasa said. 'You are travelling to Kampala with us. We are in a hurry. Don't worry. We will soon win this war against Amin. Now, stay in this vehicle. You will be safe here. We have to fight the Ugandan soldiers at Masaka.'

Major Kuchasa got out of the vehicle. Through the window I saw the smoke-blackened buildings of Mbarara, almost completely destroyed by the attack of the Tanzanian army.

On the way to Kampala, there was a lot of fighting. The Ugandan army was helped by soldiers from Libya and Palestine, and many Tanzanian soldiers died. But the Tanzanian army was stronger than the Ugandan army and, early the next evening, the seven hills of Kampala came into view.

There was much fighting during the night, and by morning the Tanzanians were in the heart of the city. I said goodbye to Major Kuchasa and thanked him for his kindness. Then I walked in the rain through the empty streets to Mulago.

The hospital was full of badly wounded soldiers. I immediately started to help Paterson and the other doctors.

Later, very tired, I walked around the city. People were stealing sugar that was hidden secretly in government buildings. There were fires everywhere. On one street, a group of angry people were attacking a man with sticks and stones.

'He worked for Amin,' somebody in the crowd explained.

Soon, I found myself outside Amin's house at Nakasero. Crowds of people were running out of the house, carrying furniture, pictures, cameras, sports equipment, telephones and radios. I pushed my way through the crowd into the house and climbed the stairs. Amin's bedroom was strangely empty. Everything was gone from the room except for some books on the shelves.

I walked to the bookshelves and pushed open the secret door. Minutes later, I was walking down the steps and along the secret passageway. It was quiet. There were no prisoners in the terrible rooms. But as I neared the room with the beds, I heard a voice. Somebody was talking!

I hid behind a door and looked into the room. I couldn't believe what I saw. On a table stood a large brown plate – and on the plate, a man's head. The hair was white with ice.

In a chair next to the table sat Idi Amin. He was wearing a large black hat and he was talking to the head.

'People say I am Hitler. Why do they say that? I am not so bad. It is true that many bad things were done in my name. But I did not know about them. But I *do* know many other things. You will not find these things in any book. They are in my head. It is the voice of God speaking to me. I know that, very soon, I will escape from here. Alive. Yes, I know many things. For example, I know that you are there, Doctor Nicholas. I can see you in the mirror. Why don't you come in and join us?'

I moved slowly into the room and stood by the table. Amin turned the plate with the head on it towards me. I saw that it was the head of one of Uganda's most important Christians.

'Are you surprised?' Amin said to me. 'I am really sorry

'I know that you are there, Doctor Nicholas.
I can see you in the mirror.'

about it. It was done without my permission. They brought me his head in an ice box. I was very angry. But that is all in the past. Tell me, why did you come back here?'

I opened my mouth to speak. But no voice came.

'I know,' Amin said. 'It is because you love me. You do not believe the bad stories about me.'

'You know there are soldiers outside?' I said. 'And crowds of people. They will kill you.'

'They love me really,' he replied calmly. 'They have forgotten. They will remember again, because I am like a father to them. But all that is history now. A new page in the story of my life is turning. I must leave them now.'

'Where will you go?'

'I have many friends around the world.'

'How will you get out?'

'I have two planes waiting for me at Nakasongola airfield.'

'But how will you get out of the city? There are Tanzanian soldiers everywhere.'

'You will help me.'

'How?'

'There is another secret passageway that comes out by the road to Entebbe. I want you to wait for me there with a vehicle. The exit from the passageway is near a big Coca Cola sign. Do you know where I mean?'

'Yes. But maybe I don't want to help you.'

'You *will* help me, Doctor Nicholas, because I am asking you. Because you are good.' He stood up and put his hand on my shoulder. 'Please help me,' he said softly.

The softness of his voice acted on me like strange medicine. He was a crazy killer, but he still had a mysterious, dreamlike power over me. I felt great pity for him. I knew then that I had to help him.

'All right,' I said. 'I will.'

Chapter 10 Escape

I borrowed a Land Rover from Major Kuchasa and drove to the secret exit on the Entebbe road. I waited by the big Coca Cola sign for an hour. Nothing happened, so I drove away.

I followed the road out of Kampala to a small village by the lake. It was empty and almost completely destroyed. I got out of the Land Rover and walked to the water. There were many small boats there. Almost without thinking, I climbed down into the biggest boat. Then I sailed slowly out onto the lake. Across the dark water, I could see lights of a far-away town in Kenya. For the first time in many years, I felt free.

Six or seven hours later, I reached the Kenyan port town of Kisumu. I went immediately to the police station. The policeman looked at me strangely. He was surprised by the green hospital clothes that I was still wearing.

'Have you got a telephone?' I asked him. 'I'd like to talk to the British Ambassador in Nairobi. I'd like to go home.'

I was taken to Nairobi in a police car, but not to the embassy. I was taken to prison. Nobody explained why.

Later that day, I was questioned by a police officer at a desk with a pile of papers in front of him.

'Why am I here?' I wanted to know.

'A few weeks ago, there was an explosion on a small plane flying from Kampala to Nairobi. Two people died. We believe that you murdered them. Do you have anything to say?'

I explained about the lion's head, but he didn't believe me. He asked me many other questions. I refused to answer any of them. Finally, he stood up.

'I am sorry, Doctor Garrigan, but we must send you back to Uganda. The new government there will want to question you about your work with Amin.'

I was returned to prison. I lay on the bed, crazy with fear and

47

unable to sleep. I remember talking to myself all night. I also remember a white man in a suit standing by my bed. He spoke to me in English, but I didn't reply. I thought it was only a dream.

The next day, I was pulled roughly from my bed and given some new clothes. I was then driven quickly to the airport and pushed onto a big passenger plane – not a plane to Uganda, a plane to England!

Many hours later, the plane landed at Gatwick Airport, south of London. I was met in the airport building by a serious-looking man who worked for the government.

'Nicholas Garrigan?' he said. 'Come with me, please.'

I followed him into a small room where, to my surprise, Nigel Stone was waiting for me.

'Hello, Garrigan,' he said.

'What do you want?' I said coldly.

'There's no need for this rudeness. You should be grateful to us. We got you out of Africa.'

I thanked him.

'But,' he added, 'we don't have to accept you back in this country.'

'What? You're joking. I'm British.'

'Not true. You're Ugandan now. You haven't got a British passport. Maybe we don't want someone like you back in our country.'

'Why?' I said. 'I have no blood on my hands.'

'There are lots of newspaper reporters outside this building, waiting to hear your story. Perhaps they will have a different opinion.'

'Then why didn't you leave me in Kenya?'

'The newspapers were getting interested.' He pushed some papers across the desk towards me. 'If you sign these papers, you can go home to Scotland without any more problems. Do you remember the money that we gave you? It's still in your bank.'

'What do these papers say?'

'That you promise not to tell the newspapers anything about British government activities in Uganda. You did everything in Uganda alone. We knew nothing about your activities.'

I signed the papers.

♦

I am now back home on a small island off the coast of Scotland. I have finished writing my story. I have tried to be honest. I still think a lot about Amin. He is often in my dreams. His name is always on the radio or TV. The Ugandan government wants Saudi Arabia to send him back. They want to punish him for his crimes.

Yesterday, while I was reading a newspaper, the phone rang.

'Hello, my good friend,' a voice said, sounding very far away. 'Is it you, Doctor Nicholas?'

I said nothing. I knew the voice very well.

'Hello? I know you can hear me,' the voice continued. 'Yes, I am here in Saudi Arabia. I got your number from a Saudi friend in London. You were always kind to me. I badly need your help. The American government wants me to help them with a problem in Iran. Khomeini, my old friend, has taken American hostages there in the American Embassy. Shall I help the American government? What do you think …?'

As he talked about his happy life in Saudi Arabia, I looked out of my window at the sea. It was quiet and beautiful and, for the first time in a long time, I felt happy. I was older and wiser now. I didn't need adventure. Finally, I put the phone down without a word and went outside. I had important work to do in my garden.

ACTIVITIES

Chapters 1–2

Before you read

1 Discuss these questions with another student.

    a Have you ever been to Africa?

       If you have, where did you go? How different is life there from in your country?

       If you haven't, which African country would you most like to visit? Why?

    b Find information about Idi Amin, a president of Uganda, in the Introduction and on the Internet. Then talk about what you have found. Was Amin a good president? Why (not)?

2 Work with another student. Have this conversation between a young doctor and one of his/her parents. End the conversation with a decision.

    Student A: You are a young doctor. You don't want a rich, comfortable life in your own country. You want to work in a poorer, foreign country. Tell your parent why.

    Student B: You are one of the doctor's parents. You don't want your son/daughter to work in a poorer, foreign country. Explain why.

3 Look at the Word List at the back of the book. Which words are:

    a for people?

    b for buildings?

    c used to talk about soldiers and fighting?

While you read

4 Finish these sentences with one of the following people.
Mabuse   Boniface Malumba   Obote   Nigel Stone
Freddy Swanepoel   Jonah Wasswa   William Waziri
Sara Zach

    a .... is Idi Amin's Minister of Health.

b .... is a South African pilot.

c .... was the president before Amin.

d .... works at the British Embassy.

e Garrigan meets .... on the bus to Mbarara.

f .... is an Israeli nursing assistant.

g .... is an African who works at the clinic.

h .... is an army officer.

After you read

5 Discuss what you know about the people in Question 4. How are they important in this part of Garrigan's story?

6 How do these people feel and why?

    a Garrigan, when he first meets Idi Amin

    b Idi Amin, about Garrigan

    c Swanepoel, about the political situation in Uganda

    d Stone, about Idi Amin

    e Garrigan, about his conversation with Stone

    f Garrigan, at the end of his first day in Mbarara

    g Waziri and Mr Malumba (Bonney's father), about Idi Amin

    h Garrigan, after lunch with the Malumba family

    i the people of Mbarara, about Idi Amin

    j Garrigan and Sara, about Amin's speech

7 Work with another student. Have this conversation between Garrigan and Sara after Amin's speech.

    Student A: You are Garrigan. You like Amin. Tell Sara why.

    Student B: You are Sara. You dislike Amin. Tell Garrigan why.

Chapters 3–4

Before you read

8 Will Garrigan be happy with life in Mbarara? Why (not)? What do you think? Write a list of reasons for and against, and compare your list with another student's.

While you read

9 Underline the correct answers.

    a Local soldiers are killed by *Obote's rebels / Amin's soldiers.*

   b Garrigan's friend Bonney is killed by *Obote's rebels / Amin's soldiers*.

   c After Gugu leaves, Sara becomes *more / less* friendly towards Garrigan.

   d Amin throws all Indian and *English / Israeli* people out of the country.

   e Garrigan becomes friendly with the British Ambassador's *secretary / wife*.

   f Campbell Amin's life *is / isn't* in danger.

   g Freddy Swanepoel is *worried / unworried* about the future.

   h Amin *enjoys / doesn't enjoy* his conversation with Garrigan and Paterson.

After you read

  10 Work with another student. Have this conversation between Doctor Merrit and Garrigan.

    Student A: You are Doctor Merrit. You want Garrigan to stay in Mbarara. Tell him why.

    Student B: You are Garrigan. You want to leave Mbarara for Kampala. Tell Doctor Merrit why.

Chapters 5–6

Before you read

  11 Discuss these questions with another student. What problems will there be for Garrigan when he next meets

   a Nigel Stone?

   b Maria Perkins?

   c Idi Amin?

While you read

  12 In which order do these happen? Number the sentences 1–10.

   a Doctor Merrit leaves Uganda. ....

   b Amin's wife dies. ....

   c Major Weir leaves Uganda. ....

   d Garrigan sees Marina with Swanepoel. ....

   e Amin is attacked. ....

f   Stone shows Garrigan some photographs.   ....

g   Amin is ill.   ....

h   Peter Mbalu-Mukasa asks Garrigan for help.   ....

i   Marina is angry with Garrigan.   ....

j   Amin writes a letter to Margaret Thatcher.   ....

After you read

13 How are these people or places important in this part of Garrigan's story?

   a   Nigel Stone

   b   Lake Victoria

   c   Marina Perkins

   d   Nakasero

   e   the Nsambya Sports Ground

   f   Willy Brandt

   g   Peter Mbalu-Mukasa

   h   the Imperial Hotel

14 Work with another student. Imagine that Garrigan has invited these people to a dinner party. He has to decide where they will sit at his round table. Each guest must be friendly with the person on each side of them. Where will Garrigan and his guests sit? Make a seating plan and then compare it with another student's plan. How successful are the two seating plans?

Doctor Merrit   Freddy Swanepoel   Nicholas Garrigan
Idi Amin   Major Weir   Marina Perkins   Nigel Stone
Peter Mbalu-Mukasa   Jonah Wasswa

Chapters 7–8

Before you read

15 What will happen when Garrigan next meets Amin? Why? Discuss your ideas.

While you read

16 Are these sentences right (✓) or wrong (✗)?

   a   Amin is invited by the Queen to visit London.   ....

   b   Garrigan's passport is stolen from his desk.   ....

c	Major Weir spied on Amin for the British Embassy.	....
d	Waziri is in a secret prison at Nakasero.	....
e	Garrigan tries to escape from Uganda.	....
f	Palestinians hijack an aeroplane from France.	....
g	Male and female hostages are kept in different rooms.	....
h	One of the hostages is taken to prison.	....
i	Amin helps the hijackers.	....
j	Sara Zach works for the Israeli army.	....

After you read

17 How does Garrigan feel and why

    a while he is driving to Nakasero?

    b while Amin is looking at his notebook?

    c while he is passing the small dark rooms in the passageway?

    d when he sees Waziri?

    e during breakfast with Amin?

    f after he arrives at Entebbe Airport?

    g when Sara speaks to him on the phone?

    h the following week, during the hostage situation?

    i when Dora Bloch is taken away from the hospital?

18 Work with another student. Have this conversation between Garrigan and Sara.

    Student A: You are Sara. You think that Garrigan is a very weak man. Talk to him about:

        • Nigel Stone's request for him to kill Amin

        • William Waziri

        • Dora Bloch's disappearance

        • your request for him to speak to Amin about the hostages. You think that Garrigan was wrong not to help in these situations. Tell him why.

    Student B: You are Garrigan. You disagree with Sara. You think that no help was possible in these situations. Tell her why.

Chapters 9–10

Before you read

19 Will the story end happily for Amin and Garrigan? Why (not)? What do you think?

While you read

20 Underline the wrong word in each of these sentences. Write the right word.

a Swanepoel is killed in an accident. ....

b Amin's army attacks Kenya. ....

c Garrigan drives to Rwanda to help Gugu. ....

d Gugu is killed by the Ugandan army. ....

e In a secret room at Nakasero, Amin is talking
to a lion's head. ....

f Garrigan tries to kill Amin. ....

g Garrigan escapes to Kenya by plane. ....

h Garrigan is taken to the embassy in Nairobi. ....

i Garrigan is put on a plane from Kenya to Uganda. ....

After you read

21 Discuss these questions with other students. What do you think?

a Garrigan says about Amin, 'He was a crazy killer but I felt great pity for him.' Why does Garrigan feel sorry for Amin? Is he right? Why (not)?

b Amin says to Garrigan, 'You love me. You do not believe the bad stories about me.' Is he right? Why (not)?

c Would Garrigan like to meet these people again? Why (not)?
Idi Amin   Sara Zach   Nigel Stone   Marina Perkins
Freddy Swanepoel   Peter Mbalu-Mukasa

d Which part of the story is
- the most exciting?
- the saddest?
- the most amusing?

22 Work with another student. Have this conversation in a Ugandan courtroom between a judge and the person who is defending Amin in court. (In fact, of course, Amin did not go to court.)

Student A: You are the judge. You think that Amin should die for his crimes. Explain why.

Student B: Your job is to defend Amin. You do not think he should die for his crimes. Tell the judge why.

23 Why is this story called *The Last King of Scotland*? Do you like the title? Why (not)? If not, can you think of a better one?

Writing

24 You are Garrigan (Chapters 4–6). What do you write about Amin in your notebook?

25 You are Nigel Stone (Chapter 7). You have just returned to England. Write a report for the British government about your stay in Uganda. Does the future of Uganda look good? Why (not)?

26 You are a reporter. Write about the hostage situation at Entebbe Airport (Chapter 8) for your newspaper.

27 You are Garrigan. Describe everything that happened on your journey from Kampala to Mbarara (Chapter 9). Give more information than there is in this book.

28 There are four 'majors' in this story: Mabuse, Weir, Zach and Kuchasa. Write four or five sentences about each of them. What are they like? What do they do for their country? How important are they to this story? Which of them do you like best? Why?

29 You are Sara Zach. Write a letter to Garrigan at his home in Scotland. Tell him about your real work in Mbarara. Why did you leave without saying goodbye?

30 You are Garrigan. You want a job as a doctor in a Scottish hospital. Write a letter to the hospital. Tell them about your work in Uganda. How useful has it been? How has it made you a better doctor?

31 You read this report in a newspaper:
Doctor Nicholas Garrigan is a bad, weak, selfish man. He was

very friendly with one of the worst murderers in African history. He did nothing to help the people of Uganda. Peter Mbalu-Mukasa, Kay Amin, Frederik Swanepoel and William Waziri all died because of him ...
Do you agree with this report? Why (not)? Write a letter to the newspaper.

32 How was life hard for the ordinary men, women and children of Uganda during the time of Idi Amin? Write about the situation, using examples from the story.

33 Imagine that Nicholas Garrigan, Sara Zachs and Nigel Stone meet for dinner in London after the end of the story. Write their conversation.

Answers for the activities in the book are available from the Penguin Readers website. A free Activity Worksheet is also available from the website. Activity Worksheets are part of the Penguin Teacher Support Programme, which also includes Progress Tests and Graded Reader Guidelines. For more information, please visit: www.penguinreaders.com.

WORD LIST

abortion (n) the ending of a baby's life by a doctor before it is born

ambassador (n) an important person who works for his or her government in another country, in his or her country's **embassy**

army (n) a country's soldiers

border (n) the line between two countries

bungalow (n) a house with only one floor and no stairs

clinic (n) a place, smaller than a hospital, where sick people go for help

cow (n) an animal that people keep for its milk or meat

explosive (n) something that makes a sudden loud noise. It can destroy buildings and kill people around it. This action is an **explosion**.

hijack (n/v) the taking of an aeroplane or other vehicle in the middle of its journey by a group of people with guns

hostage (n) the prisoner of someone who wants something. When he or she gets it, the prisoner is (sometimes) freed.

lion (n) a large wild cat from Africa

major (n) an army officer

minister (n) an important person in a country's government

passageway (n) a long, narrow area with walls on both sides

power (n) the ability of a person to make decisions about other people's lives; something that can change you. When a person or group of people **take power** in a country, they form a new government, with or without the people's agreement.

rebel (n) a person who fights against the government

servant (n) someone who works in another person's house

situation (n) everything that is happening at one time in one place

uniform (n) special clothes that are worn by everyone in a group. Soldiers and nurses wear uniforms, for example.

wounded (adj) badly hurt in a fight or a war